Grandpa, Is That You?

Written by
Mary Edwards-Olson

Illustrated by January Tankersley

To everyone that has watched a
loved one slip away from them
through lost memories and empty stares.
You are strong and not alone!

Grandpa, Is that You?
Written by Mary Edwards-Olson
Illustrated by January Tankersley
Published January 2019
Skippy Creek
Imprint of Jan-Carol Publishing, Inc

Copyright © Mary Edwards-Olson
ISBN: 978-1-945619-91-5
Library of Congress Control Number: 2019932009

You may contact the publisher:
Jan-Carol Publishing, Inc
PO Box 701
Johnson City, TN 37605
publisher@jancarolpublishing.com
jancarolpublishing.com

Jan-Carol
Publishing, Inc
"every story needs a book"

Letter to the Reader

This story, like my last, was inspired by my beautiful mother, who lost her fight with Alzheimer's on October 23, 2017. My children watched their beloved Nana slip away, but through their compassion and strength they helped me create this beautiful book. I hope this book brings comfort to those who read it. My advice would be: continue to love those who suffer, make it a point to include them in your daily life, and remember their memory is fading and days are hard. But they are still the person you love.

Acknowledgments

Thank you to everyone that has walked beside me as I continue to fight to find a cure! I am so blessed to be part of such an amazing community, loving family, and understanding friend group! Your support has truly helped make a change in so many people's lives! Thank you to Tracey W.; because of your hard work and dedication to helping those in need, many have found hope, knowledge, and compassion! You truly are the definition of compassion and self-lessness. To January T. and Janie J., thank you both for believing in me and understanding my passion. Without you, my book would just be words.

Grandpa, is that you?
Do you remember me?

And all the fun things
we used to do and see?

Like fishing, camping, and climbing trees.

Or flying kites, swimming,
and running from bees.

Your memory is gone, and your smile is too!

You're not the same Grandpa
I thought I knew.

But that's okay
because I love you so!

I'll do whatever I can
to let you know.

I understand Alzheimer's is like a grumpy gray cloud!

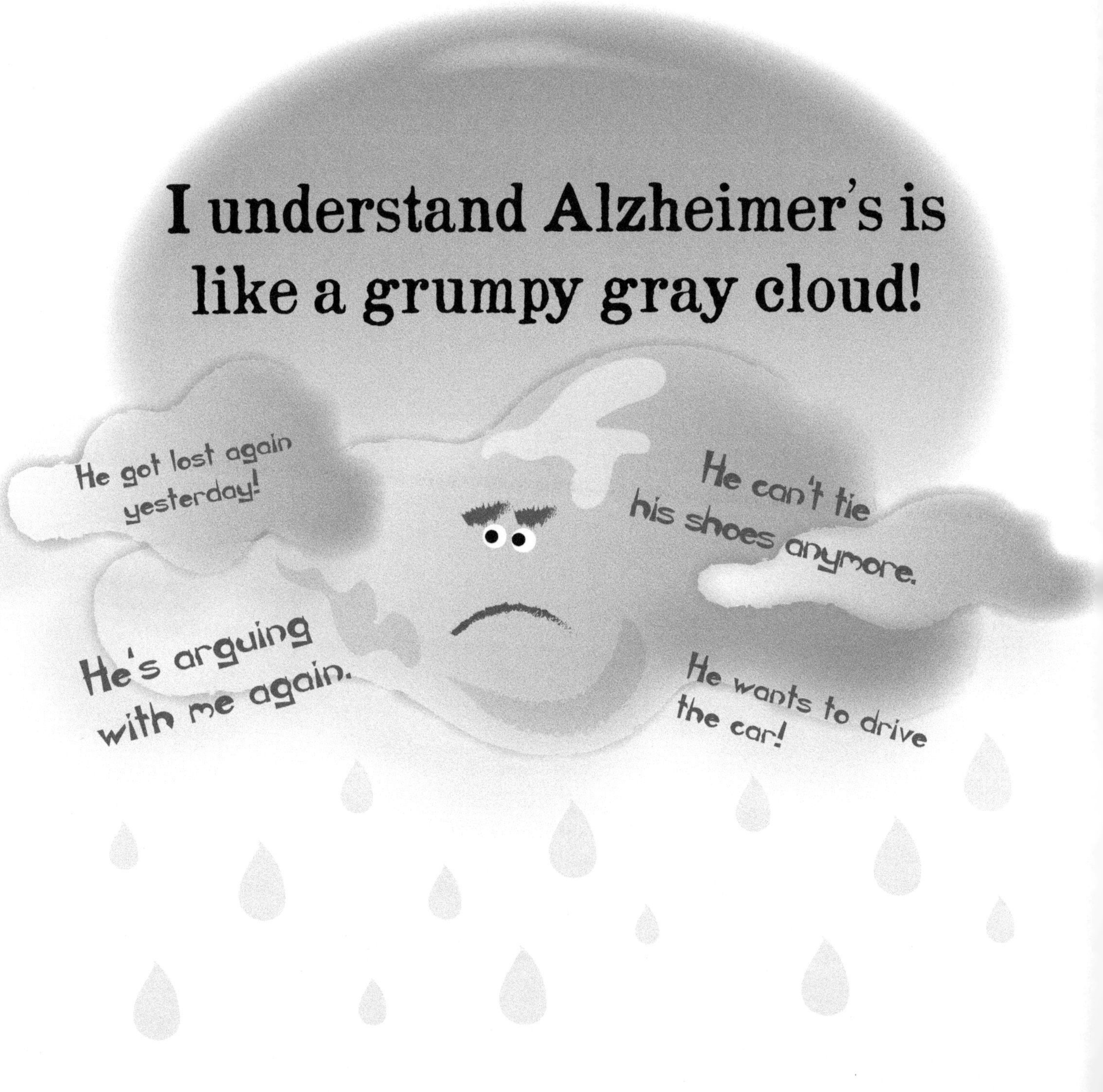

It covers your brain and makes you less proud.

You feel lost and confused
in your everyday life.

You may even forget your kids and your wife.

But I am here to tell you,
you are always safe and sound.

No matter how bad your days get, I'll always be around.

Hurry under the umbrella!

...and you can come to baseball and watch me play.

I'll introduce you to every one of my friends...

...but that's just because
your personality
will change.

Alzheimer's disease takes more than just your memories, it's true.

It takes **your independence**,
smile, **and sadly**, **your life too.**

So, for now, tell me the stories as we camp in the woods...

...of how you played ball with your friends in your old neighborhood.

And if you forget my bedtime story I will help you fill in the blank...

...of magic and pirates
who must walk the plank.

So remember, Grandpa,
please do not cry!

And on those days when you are too weak or too sick...

...I'll take care of you, love you,
and still be your sidekick.

Know that my love will always be true.

Even if I forget
and ask,
"Grandpa, is that you?"

About the Author

I wake up every day wanting to give up and crawl into a hole, but my drive to find a cure overpowers this emotion. I fight, and I refuse to stop! I talk constantly about my journey, the need for a cure, and the pain the hopeless carry. I am a voice and I refuse to be silenced! I released my first children's book in 2017. It was named on the Amazon Hot New Release list, as well as winning a 4-star award through the ATAI book contest. I'm honored by my numerous writeups in local newspapers and in national blogs, television appearances, and for being named community hero twice for my commitment to fight Alzheimer's. I'm a proud member of the group Alzheimer's Authors, as well a guest blogger on sites that focus on Alzheimer's and its effects on patients and their families.

Author Q & A:

Q: Why do you center your books around Alzheimer's?

A: I wrote *When the Sun Shines Through* because of my personal journey. I was a caregiver for my mother and watched first hand as Alzheimer's slowly stole her from us.

Q: What was it like being a care giver?

A: Caring for my mother was a roller coaster of emotions. You go from crying so hard that every inch of your body aches to being so overwhelmed with joy when a piece of them peeks through the mask of Alzheimer's. I was ignorant to this disease and its cruelty until I watched it slowly take my mother, piece by piece.

Q: What advice do you have for others who find themselves in similar situations?

A: Please remember it's the disease. Your loved one is in there, scared and confused. Show compassion, and remember to take time for yourself. As a caregiver, we often take a back seat, but remember your loved one needs you to be happy and emotionally and physically healthy. They may not express it, but they understand.

CPSIA information can be obtained
at www.ICGtesting.com
Printed in the USA
LVHW072349240519
619076LV00002B/2/P

9 781945 619915